Twisted Tales

By Lynn & Darryl Porrino

Darryl Porrino

Lynn Porrino

Copyright © 2015 L & D Porrino

All rights reserved, including the right to reproduce this book, or portions thereof in any form.

ISBN-13:978-1502910318

by Lynn & Darryl Porrino

Cover designed by Lynn & Darryl Porrino

A collection of short stories written by Lynn & Darryl Porrino. They are based on a theme of horror, revenge and the unexpected. With a nod to the classic tales of horror and the traditions of Hammer and Amicus.

Contents

		Page
1.	Midnight Journey	7
2.	His And Hearse	13
3.	Dead Man's Hand	17
4.	The Red Shoes	21
5.	Stranger On The Shore	25
6.	The Gravedigger	31
7.	The Phone Box	33
8.	The Mirror	37
9.	The Ghost Walk	41
10.	The Maze	47
11.	The Unknown Soldier	53
12.	Neat And Tidy	59
13.	The Tower	66
14.	The Cyclist	70
15.	The Vicarage	75
16.	Comrades In Arms	81
17.	The Miner	85

Midnight Journey

On a cold clear night Doctor Henry James found himself walking along a lonely deserted road. It was early January 1899. The moon hung full and bright over the hills, illuminating the country road, the bare trees glistening in the moonlight. Up ahead he saw the welcoming sight of the local railway station, lit up by lamplight. He walked briskly up to the entrance. Smoke spiraled up from the chimney into the still night air.

Dr James opened the waiting room door and peered in. There was a large roaring fire burning in the grate, a single bench lining the wall opposite. Beside the fire was the ticket office window. Suddenly the chiming of the clock as it struck 11pm broke the silence. Beneath the clock was an old tattered map of the rail network, the bottom corner torn and hanging down. The ticket office window was open but there was nobody inside.

Henry stepped through the opposite door which led out onto the platform. The last train to London was waiting patiently, steam hissing from the engine, as it looked into the dark tunnel entrance. He looked around for signs of life but could find nobody, not even the stationmaster who he knew to be a permanent fixture at the station. He wandered back into the waiting room and went into the ticket office. On the table in the corner of the office was a table and two chairs. A teapot and a mug of steaming hot tea were standing on the table. "Anybody about?" he called but went unanswered. " I can't miss this train" he muttered. "I have an important appointment with the Duke Of Clarence at my Harley Street surgery in the morning."

He had a practice in the fashionable London district, consisting mainly of people of distinction. He also performed minor operations on poorer people now and again, as a gesture of goodwill and to raise his reputation.

He left his fare on the table and selected a ticket to London. He again wandered out onto the platform. He strolled to the end of the platform by the engine, and, under the solitary gas lamp he peered into the mouth of the tunnel, hoping to catch a glimpse of the driver, but he couldn't see anyone. Under the lamplight, in his frock coat and top hat, he appeared to be the only passenger for the late express.

Henry opened the door to the first class carriage and climbed in. No sooner had he seated himself the train lurched forward and began to move. The engine began to puff and grunt as the speed increased. It disappeared into the tunnel as it gained momentum. Henry opened the carriage door and looked out into the corridor. There was no sign of any other passengers and not even the conductor appeared. The train sped through the tunnel, which seemed endless. Henry went back into his compartment and sat down. He took out his newspaper and glanced through it.

Gradually the train began to slow down. Henry got up from his seat and opened the window. He leaned out and looked forward. Although the train was still in the tunnel, a station appeared up ahead. The well-lit platform came into view as the train halted. Henry got off the train and stepped onto the platform. At the end of the platform was a tall, sinister figure. He was dressed in a black suit, black hat and gloves and black shoes. He was intently reading a newspaper. Henry walked up to him. " I say sir, where are we?" he asked. The man never looked up, but just kept reading his newspaper. " Welcome Dr James we have been expecting you." he said in a low menacing voice. " How do you know my name?" asked Henry. "I know all the passengers who alight at this station, you are a trifle late though." Henry was dumbounded. "How can I be late when I was not intending to come here?"

"My dear fellow, do you not yet realise your fate?" As the stranger said this he finally looked up. Henry gasped and stumbled backwards, horrified at the sight that met his eyes. The face staring back at him was not alive. He had a sallow complexion, made worse by the hollow sunken cheeks. His eyes were pools of pitch black, as if they had been removed. His thin pale lips opened slightly to reveal two rows of decaying stumps that were once teeth. His long bony arm reached out to Henry and offered him the newspaper. Henry tentatively took the proffered paper and looked at the headlines.

"Fatal train crash on the mainline, no survivors" ran the headline. Henry glanced further down the story until he came to a list of the dead. There were six names on the list and he knew them all. Five were poor patients of his who had died on the operating table in suspicious circumstances. The sixth name was the one that shocked him the most. " Doctor Henry James the Harley Street specialist was also one of the casualties."

"This must be some kind of joke!" he shouted.

"Oh no sir" said the sinister man in black, "You have reached the end of your journey. Please step this way." Henry followed him into the waiting room. Inside were five figures seated on a bench opposite. They were all in various stages of decomposition. They looked up as he walked in. They were like walking zombies, undead cadavars, creatures of his darkest nightmares.

"Welcome doctor, we have been expecting you" said one of them. Henry glanced across at the putrid figure that spoke to him and saw that it spat out teeth and phlegm as it spoke. He recognised it as one of the five patients that had died needlessly at his hands.

"What do you want of me!" he screamed.

The creature shuffled towards him and shook his head as he did so. As he did this one of his eyes fell out of it's socket. He caught it in his bony hand and held it up to Dr James.

"Oh I'd say it's an eye for an eye at last."

As he said this the four other figures rose slowly and shuffled towards him. Horrified by this sight he backed away from them. Slowly they came forward, loose flecks of skin falling from their bodies as they moved. Henry found himself cornered and turned to the sinister figure in black.

"Please help me!" he cried out, but the figure just smiled and shook his head. Henry's last sight was that of a calloused , bony hand, skin hanging loose, as the fingers slowly reached out towards his eyes. He fainted before the end.

The train slowly left the station as it returned to the land of the living in search of it's next victim.

His And Hearse

Six years, that's how long we've been married. Just look at where we are now. Our business is death, we deal with it every day. We run our own undertakers business, Jan and me. We started it just before we got married. We're doing quite nicely out of death and now death is going to do quite nicely out of us.

It all started to go wrong last summer. Jan was having trouble with her car, a battered old Renault, and she took it to a garage in New Street. That's where she met him, Johnny Jackson, that slimy toad of a car mechanic. It took me quite a while to figure it out. Those subtle changes in Jan's manner, the unexplained absences from home, and her reluctance to join me in the marital bed, claiming to sleep better in the spare room.

Then one day I came home from work unexpectedly early. I was not surprised to find that Jan was not there to greet me. However, I soon realised that I was not alone after all. There were voices coming from upstairs, did we have burglars? Slowly I crept up the stairs not knowing what would be up there to greet me. The voices were coming from "our" bedroom. I gently pushed the door open just a little and peered in. There they were, Jan and Johnny, naked in our bed, cuddled up together. They were so wrapped up in each other that they never noticed me. They were laughing and joking together, my slut of a wife and that damned grease monkey, finding it funny that they were making a monkey out of me. They then discussed leaving and making a new life together, once she had robbed me of my fortune.

I crept out of the room, down the stairs and out of the front door, my mind in turmoil. If anybody was going to lose everything it certainly wasn't going to be me. Slowly but surely a plan formed in my mind. Life carried on as normal, or so Jan thought.

We found ourselves quite busy over the coming months. I had taken over driving the hearse after Sid, our driver, had managed to get himself banned for drink driving. I had to take a coffin down the steep country lane to the chapel of rest but the brakes were playing up and they needed fixing. Jan offered to take the hearse to the garage on New Street to be fixed. I knew her real reason for wanting to go there but said nothing.

That evening I decided to put my plan in action. I moved the long rug from the hallway and put it on the polished wooden floor on the landing.

Later that night, as usual, Jan got up and headed downstairs for her late night drop of scotch. I got up and followed her onto the landing. As she got to the top of the stairs I cried out, "be careful Jan!". Startled, she turned round to face me. As she did so she became unbalanced. The rest was easy. I just pulled the rug from under her feet and down she went tumbling down a long flight of stairs. I even heard her neck snap as she hit the floor.

An unfortunate accident was how the coroner described it. I was beside myself with grief. Jan's family had come round to give me moral support. I was determined to give my wife the send off she deserved. The arrangements were made and it was decided that Jan's final resting place would be the family vault in the cemetery at the foot of the steep country lane. I was to drive her to her final resting place.

As I drove the hearse to the top of the hill I could see the granite entrance to the vault down below. I eased the hearse over the hill and down the other side. Looking over my shoulder towards the coffin I told Jan that she would be all alone now. Better slow things down here, the hill was quite steep at this point. I dabbed on the brakes. Nothing happened so I pressed harder. Still there was no response. I frantically stamped on the brakes with no response. The speed increased dramatically. The hearse was heading for the oak tree at the bottom of the hill.

It was in those final moments that I realised that Jan had got those brakes fixed after all. Johnny Jackson had fixed them all right. Now here I was trapped in a hearse with a coffin. I was in a coffin of my own.

The speed increased in spite of my desperate attempts to change down through the gears. Brace yourself lad this is your final moment.

The newspaper headlines described how a grieving husband was cruelly robbed of his life as he was taking his late wife to her final resting place. The impact of the car hitting the tree was so fierce that the coffin had been thrown forward and the driver's head had been decapitated by the coffin lid and had come to rest in the coffin beside his late wife. We started this business together and we ended it together.

Dead Man's Hand

Jack awoke with a start as the bright sunshine hit his face through the hospital window. For a moment he couldn't think where he was and then he grimaced as his actions came flooding back, and then the pain , the like of which he could never imagine possible. As he looked around the room and then down at his new hand a tear rolled down his cheek. The doctors had told him that a young man had been killed and they had used one of his hands for the transplant. They knew nothing of the young man, he could have been anyone, but Jack was grateful to him anyway. No friends or relatives of the young man had come forward.

The surgeon said it would be a long job getting used to the new hand. There would be more operations, tests and physio. By the time all that was done they said he wouldn't be able to tell that he had a new hand. He knew he would never forget what had happened. He had been on the combine harvester. It was five o'clock and he still had half an acre to finish. He was supposed to be meeting Maisie tonight and he didn't want to be late. She was a gorgeous blonde, blue eyed with curves in all the right places. She was every boys dream. Well all the boys in the village dreamed of her. He could see her big blue eyes, her pouting lips, teasing him.

Then bang, the combine had stopped. He jumped down and went to inspect the damage. A large root had got jammed in the blades. He cursed, thinking would he never be finished.

Of course he didn't switch the machine off. Stupid, stupid, stupid thing to do. He had grown up on the farm and it was drummed into him, switch off any machinery before doing any work on them. All he could think of though was Maisie. He saw the problem and reached in to clear the blockage.

The doctors said he was lucky that it was a clean cut and his hand had been severed as if by a surgeon. They couldn't have done a better job themselves.

He must have passed out, all he could remember was his dad trying to wake him. He then felt the pain, the like of which he never wanted to experience again.

He was being discharged from hospital today. He would be going back to the farm, but would only be doing light duties for some time to come. The doctors were very pleased with the hand. They said there was a lot of strength in the fingers. He was able to squeeze things quite easily. In fact he thought if these fingers were around someone's neck he could very easily squeeze the life out of them.

His brother Joe came to pick him up. By the time they got back to the farm he had had enough of the hand jokes. He had the crazy urge to strangle Joe to shut him up.

The only bright spot in the day was the fact that he would be seeing Maisie tonight for the first time since before the accident, so maybe he could put up with the teasing for now. Maisie came early to pick him up. They drove to the end of the country lane and stopped. It was then that Maisie dropped her bombshell. She was seeing someone else. In fact they were already engaged. He was devastated. The only thing keeping him going was the thought of seeing Maisie again. He began to feel angry. She tried to explain to him why she didn't want him, but he knew. It was his new hand. It revolted her. He watched her talk without listening. He watched her red lips move, becoming more of a sneer by the minute. He felt his new fingers tingle, itching to grab her round the neck and strangle the life out of her.

As he walked back up the lane to the farmhouse he looked at his new hand. He was amazed at just how strong the hand was.

Joe walked up the lane towards the farm. These early mornings were great, with perfect silence, just the bird song to break it. As he walked on he saw Maisie's car parked at the verge. There was somebody inside, they looked asleep. As he peered in he got the shock of his life. It was Maisie sat there. The once pretty Maisie, with her tongue hanging out of her mouth and her eyes bulging. She had red marks around her neck, like finger marks. It was obvious she was dead.

He rushed up to the farmhouse and opened the door to the kitchen. The sight that greeted him was like something out of a horror film. His parents were lying on the kitchen floor, both strangled, as was his sister. On the far side of the room was his brother Jack, also dead. He had cut off his new hand with a carving knife and had bled to death. The hand that had given life had now taken life.

The Red Shoes

It was pay day today and Selina was going out in her lunch break to buy the red shoes she had seen last week. They were red , four inch heels and a nice strap around the ankle. It would mean very little left from her wages but Billy was worth it. She was determined she would be his wife before the year was out. She hated it at home with her mum, who was always getting her to do things around the house. She would make sure that when she was Billy's wife she would never lift a finger. Life was for living and she was going to make sure she lived hers. She was going to sit in her chair all day painting her nails and reading her magazines, and then party all night.

Billy was a good catch, his father owned the print works where her father worked. That's how she came to meet him. Her father had left his lunch behind one morning and Selina's mother made her take them to him at work. When she walked into his office Billy was there. She could see he was smitten straightaway. As she was leaving he rushed after her and asked her if she would go to the pictures with him. Of course she said yes. She could see the advantage of going out with the bosses son. They lived on the other side of town, in a big posh house in it's own grounds, not in a tatty terrace like her. She was made for better things, she was going places, and with her looks she could have her pick of boys. She was a petite brunette with curves in all the right places. She knew the effect she had on the local boys, but she wanted better. She had seen the look of lust in Billy's eyes but she wouldn't let things go too far, not until she got a ring on her finger.

It was a great relief to her to hear the buzzer sound for the lunch break. She hoped the red shoes would still be there. She had already tried them on and they were a perfect fit, and red was Billy's favourite colour. The shoes were still there waiting for her. She bought them and rushed back to work. It was a long afternoon and she was relieved to be clocking off at 5. It was Friday and there was a dance on at the Palace. Billy was picking her up at 7.30 and she wanted to be ready and perfect by then.

Billy had been thinking of Selina all day. In fact it was all he could think of. He knew that Selina secretly wanted him to propose to her, it was obvious really. He wasn't ready to settle down yet and when he was it wouldn't be with someone like her. She was good fun to be with but he would marry someone of his own class.

He arrived at Selina's house, and knocked on the door. She opened it and his eyes nearly popped out of his head. The red dress she had on was positively indecent, and the shoes were great. Tonight was going to be his night he thought to himself. Selina was a tease and she knew the effect she had on men. If the looks on the other blokes at the Palace were anything to go by she was a stunner all right.

They spent a great night dancing together but as the night wore on Selina's feet started to hurt. The straps of her shoes were starting to cut into her ankles. As soon as we get in the car these shoes are coming off, she thought. They left the dance and got in the car. Selina tried to undo the straps on her shoes but they wouldn't unfasten. They were getting tighter and really hurting. Billy was busy trying to kiss her. "Stop it Billy and try to help me get these shoes off, they're killing me!" Billy tried to undo the straps but he couldn't. He got out his penknife and tried to cut them off but the straps were too tough and the knife didn't even leave a mark. By this time Selina was in real pain and started screaming. Billy started to panic and then decided to take her to the hospital. They got to the hospital in minutes. Billy carried Selina into the hospital and got a nurse. She quickly rushed them in to see a doctor.

The doctor looked at the red shoes on those black feet. It was a pity he couldn't get them off and had no option than to amputate the poor girl's feet.

Selina always wanted to spend her days sat in a chair doing her nails and reading her magazines. Well now she had a chair of her own, only this one had wheels.

Stranger On The Shore

Leaving the office on Friday night for the last time for a full month was a good feeling despite the rain teeming down. Donna thought the weather matched her mood perfectly. It was the last straw to what had been a long stressful and emotional year that had started with a messy divorce and then discovering the pile of debt James had left behind to sort out. Well sort it out she had. It had left her homeless and penniless but now she was debt free and could start again. She was going to move in with her sister for now. She had stood by her throughout the whole business, getting her through all the dark days. Her sister had encouraged her to get away for a while and totally relax. Donna had taken up her suggestion and had rented a cottage in the seaside village of Pennington. She could put all her problems behind her and return full of hope for a new better future.

So here she was, driving down to the coast, looking forward to getting some fresh sea air. She arrived at Pennington and drove down the seafront to a row of five cottages, all holiday lets. Hers was the last one. The letting agency had agreed to leave a key under the plant pot for her. She opened the front door and stepped in. It was a plain and simple cottage with two bedrooms, kitchen, bathroom and living room. Donna put her suitcase on the bed and headed for a shower. She then went downstairs and opened the fridge. There was a bottle of wine waiting for her. She opened it and went into the living room, sat down and poured herself a glass of wine. She began to unwind at last.

The next morning dawned bright and sunny. Donna looked at the travel alarm clock she brought with her. It was half past ten. Her stomach rumbled, reminding her that she hadn't eaten since the previous afternoon. She showered and dressed and then ventured outside. She went down to the row of shops she saw yesterday. There was a village store, a bakery, a cafe and a few souvenir shops, just enough to keep her occupied. She wandered along the seafront taking in the fresh sea air. After the noise and smell of London this was great, she thought. She stopped and looked down the beach. At the far end was an elderly man in a black overcoat and black trilby. He saw her looking and lifted his hat. She waved back and then turned and walked away. She was not ready to get into conversation with anyone just yet.

Donna walked back to the cafe and went in. She sat at a window table. The girl in the cafe came and took her order. When she returned she became quite chatty and told Donna of attractions and places to visit. She also told Donna about the old gent she had seen on the front. He was Henry, a widower, who walked along the seafront every day. He would pop into the village store for his morning paper and then go to the cafe for tea and toast and a read of the paper. He lived in one of the old fisherman's cottages just off the front. She said he was a nice quiet man. His wife had died in childbirth, leaving him to bring up their daughter Annabel alone. Tragedy struck again three years ago. His daughter was out walking on the beach near the rock pools. She was never seen again and it was believed that she had gotten stuck in the quicksands near the rock pools and got dragged under. It was a treacherous spot if you didn't know exactly where the quicksands were. Annabel must have lost her bearings.

Donna left the cafe and called into the village store for supplies. She then headed home and made a light lunch for herself. She then went for a walk on the front, making a mental note not to go near the rock pools. She then went home, watched a weepy movie, had a late dinner and then went to bed. This set the pattern for the next couple of weeks.

It was the middle of the third week that thing started to go downhill. She had stopped up later than normal to watch a film. It was about a couple that were splitting up, and all the bad memories came flooding back. She got really upset and opened a bottle of wine. She kept pouring glass after glass and before she knew it she was on a second bottle. She stumbled upstairs to the bedroom and collapsed on the bed.

She woke up the following morning with a massive hangover. Her head was pounding unmercifully. She showered, got dressed and went out to the village store for some tablets to cure her headache. She decided to go to the cafe for some strong black coffee. As she entered the cafe she saw Henry, the old man she saw on the seafront every morning, sat at a table. He introduced himself and asked her to join him. They got chatting and they agreed to meet every morning in the cafe. This routine carried on until Donna found herself in her last few days of her holiday. In a way she was glad to be going back to London. She felt a lot calmer and stronger than she had for quite a while and felt she was ready to rejoin the hustle and bustle of city life. Henry had invited her to his house for a home cooked meal that evening and she readily accepted. They had become firm friends these past weeks. She suspected he just needed company as he had been alone for the past three years. She only ate a light lunch so she could fully appreciate Henry's cooking. She went round to his house at 7 o'clock. He had promised her a roast beef dinner with a special pudding to follow. She was quite hungry by now and ready to sit and eat. The meal was lovely and they had a good chat about their respective lives. Henry talked a lot about his wife and his daughter Annabel. She was 28 when she died and was single and still living at home. He had never quite got over her sad death.

They finished the meal and Donna said her farewells and left, promising to meet Henry in the cafe the following morning.

The following morning Donna was up early and, feeling energetic, she decided to see how far she could walk down the beach. She set off and headed towards the rock pools. As she got closer to the rocks she spotted Henry sitting on them looking out to sea. He turned and saw her, and beckoned her to him. She walked towards him only to see him get up and walk behind the rocks. She followed him behind the rocks and saw him sitting by the rock pools. "Come and join me" he said and indicated a safe path avoiding the quicksands. Donna followed his directions but quickly found herself stuck in the soft sinking sand. As she struggled to free herself she only managed to sink further in. She called to Henry to help her but he just watched and smiled. She sunk deeper and she called out frantically for help just before she disappeared forever.

Henry watched her go under and smiled. "See Annabel, I told you I would bring a friend to keep you company, make her welcome." He strolled off to the cafe for a fish and chip lunch. He always had a good appetite when he took a new friend down to the beach for Annabel.

The Gravedigger

Albert looked around him for the last time and gave a sigh. He had spent most of his life in this cemetery digging graves. He had started as a boy, as had his father before him. He was 70 now and it was finally time to hang up his shovel. Still he had got his last souvenir today. He had it wrapped up in his pocket. Tomorrow he would take it down to his allotment and put it in his shed with the rest of his collection. He was going to the pub now for a last pint with his fellow gravediggers. He wasn't too bothered really but they meant well. It was their way of saying goodbye. He had taught them how to do the job and they had been good pupils. He didn't drink as a rule, as his mother had drunk herself to death, always having a gin bottle in her hand. She always blamed him and his father for her problems. She married Albert's father at 16. SheShe was well known as a drunk around the Her father was glad to be rid of her, having five other daughters and two sons it was one less mouth to feed. When Albert was born she made the sign of the cross. He was born with a club foot. It was then that she hit the gin, saying she was being punished for all her sins and by the time he was seven she was dead. Albert's father never remarried. Well who else would want the devil's child in their house, for that was what the locals called Albert. He was teased unmercifully at school and left there friendless. He was spat at in the street and people crossed the road to avoid him. Yes his club foot was the cause of all his problems and all the abuse and mockery he received. He left school and became a gravedigger with his father. He loved the job and was a quick learner. After his father died Albert was left to live and work on his own. It was about this time that he got his allotment. When he wasn't at work he was busy on his allotment growing all kinds of vegetables. He built a shed out of old bits of wood he found lying around. He kept all his tools in there. That was when he got the idea of collecting his souvenirs as he could fix up some shelves to display them. He was very nervous when he got the first one and was sweating profusely as he took it back to the shed, hoping nobody would notice. After that it was quite easy and he soon built up quite a collection.

He supposed that now he was retiring he should get rid of his collection but he couldn't bring himself to do it, after all it was a perfect collection and he was proud of it. He had just the one pint as he wanted to get to the allotment before dark. He kept touching it in his pocket. It was a beauty and would just finish off his large collection. He got to the shed and got out a jar and put the souvenir in. He put it on the shelf with all the others. It was on the shelf along with a row of jars full of perfect little feet that he had amputated from the little kids he had buried. He did so admire perfect feet.

The Phone Box

Phone boxes, everyday objects, ubiquitous, functional, invisible. How many people never give a second glance to the old red phone box? Nobody noticed them come, and nobody notices them go. They were relics of a bygone age. Now mobiles, that was the future. Well life and death is important, and that old red phone box could be a lifesaver. At least that's what one man once thought.

He was on a touring holiday in the Scottish Highlands. He had an important phone call to make but couldn't get a signal on his mobile.

"Damn, I must make this call, I need to find a landline. He drove into a remote little village. Nothing much there, the usual quaint cottages, pub and tacky souvenir shops. In a quiet corner of the village square stood an old red phone box, it's door slightly ajar.

"Great, I'll use that phone."

He stepped into the phone box and the door immediately closed behind him. He tried to use the phone but it appeared to be out of order.

"Damn" he thought, "What do I do now?"
He turned towards the door and pushed it. The door, however, wouldn't move. Even the full weight of his thirteen stone frame wouldn't budge it.

"What the hell is wrong with this door!"

After struggling vainly for ten minutes he stopped to take a breather. A group of young lads came by and he called them over to help him. They all tried to open the door as he pushed from the other side but it just wouldn't move. The lads just shrugged their shoulders and walked off.

Just then a couple of workmen came by. They tried to open the door and even used a crowbar but to no avail. "We'll get you some help" one of them said and they walked into the pub. "Please hurry it's getting quite stuffy in here". He was beginning to panic. He took off his jacket, loosened his tie and sat on the floor of the box.

After about fifteen minutes a lorry bearing a phone company logo drove into the village square. Two men got out and surveyed the scene.

"Please can you help" cried the stranger.

The two men didn't say anything. They backed the lorry up to the phone box. They loosened the bolts holding the phone box to it's concrete base. They hooked the box up to the crane and lifted it onto the back of the lorry.

"What are you doing!" he cried but they never answered, just got back into the cab and drove off.

"They must be taking me to the depot to use specialist equipment" he thought.

They drove out of the village and into the remote countryside. The journey seemed to take ages. They climbed up into the mountains. They stopped at a crossroads. Coming the other way was another lorry also carrying a phone box, but this one was empty. They carried on an a little further up the road they caught up with another lorry with a phone box on it. This one was occupied by a young girl. She stood sobbing uncontrollably. She saw him in his box and looked imploringly at him.

Their journey continued until they turned off onto a small track. This came to an end at the entrance of a tunnel that had a security gate over the entrance. The lorries never slowed down, the gate opened automatically to let them in. The tunnel was well lit but as they approached a large cavern they went out, only the dimmed lights of the lorries giving any light. They hoisted the phone box off the lorry and the men in the second lorry did the same with the girl's box. They then drove back out through the tunnel leaving them in total darkness.

Suddenly the lights came on, illuminating the whole cavern. The sight that greeted the stranger was absolutely shocking and horrific. He gasped at the terror that met his eyes, and, realising the futility and hopelessness of his situation, he sank to his knees and wept. "Oh god no, don,t leave me here!" he cried despairingly. He looked imploringly at the girl in the other phone box. She sobbed uncontrollably as she too saw the horror that was laid out before her. Her gaze drifted out towards the sight before her, not understanding how this could be happening.

Just then the lights went out and they were once more plunged into darkness.

It was the last thing that they ever saw. Hundreds of red phone boxes packed tightly together, as far as the eye could see. Each one occupied by people. Some were alive, some only just so, their torment clearly visible on their tortured faces. Some long dead, in various stages of decomposition. Some had scratched the glass in a futile attempt to get out, but their fingers bled and blood smeared all down the glass. Some , in fragile mental states, had bashed their heads against the doors, their brains covering the glass. Others had strangled themselves with the phone cords and others had torn out their eyes in despair. Not one occupant had managed to escape.

The haunting sounds of the tortured souls pierced the still air. No hope, no escape, just a slow lingering death.

In a quiet corner of a village square stood an old red phone box, it's door slightly ajar.

The Mirror

Charles King QC, that was his title. He had been a judge for the last twenty odd years and then was forced to retire due to his high blood pressure and dicky heart. He was glad in a way to finally put his working life behind him and try to enjoy his retirement. He had dealt with a lot of tough cases in his career, some guilty, some not. He always enjoyed his job as a judge especially when the jury found someone guilty, on his direction, wether they were guilty or not. He got great pleasure in handing out long custodial sentences, the longer the better. It kept the scum off the streets for decent people to feel safe again. He knew he had been a bit harsh but he didn't regret a minute of it. Still, that was in the past and it was time to relax with his wife Mary.

They sold their large house in the country and moved into a large flat in a fashionable area of London. And so it began. For the next ten years they furnished their flat with antiques that they found at auctions and antique fairs. They built up quite a collection of expensive furniture, porcelain and silver. They kept most of it and sold some on. They had got the flat just about how they wanted it. There was just one item they wanted but couldn't agree on. That was a mirror. They saw quite a few but dismissed them one after another as they couldn't agree on which one to have.

Then one day Mary started complaining of feeling unwell. A trip to the doctors and a few tests and it was confirmed that she had cancer. It was a big blow to them both. There followed an operation and a series of chemotherapy. Mary was finally given the all clear and life resumed as normal, antique hunting again. Just when things were looking up Mary had the bombshell that the cancer was back and with a vengeance. There was nothing that could be done this time and Mary eventually died.

Charles was left on his own to carry on. Gradually he settled again into his life. One morning the phone rang. He couldn't be bothered answering it and let the answerphone kick in. It was Mr Reid, owner of an antique shop he and Mary had visited many times and bought various items. He left a message saying he had found the ideal mirror for him. He called Mr Reid back about half an hour later, not wanting to appear too keen. Mr Reid had always known just what he and Mary were looking for and so he was intrigued to see this mirror. He arranged to go to the shop later that morning, after he had his breakfast and read of the morning papers.

Charles set off later that morning, with some trepidation, to Mr Reid's shop. He entered the shop and the bell tinkled as he opened the door. Mr Reid appeared out of the back room. "Hello Mr King, how nice to see you. The mirror is in the back room. Come this way and I'll show it to you."

Charles went with Mr Reid into the back room. He didn't get his hopes up as they had struggled to find the right mirror over the years and this might not fit the bill. There on the table was a large object, hidden under a blanket. Mr Reid slowly lifted it to reveal the mirror. Charles couldn't believe his eyes. The mirror was absolutely perfect, just what he and Mary had been looking for all these years. They agreed a price and Charles paid there and then. Delivery was arranged for the following morning. He took one final look at the mirror before he left. He thought for a minute that there was the face of a man in the bottom left hand corner of the mirror, but it couldn't be real, just a trick of the light he thought.

He left the shop and walked home, thinking of the sad melancholic face he thought he had seen in the mirror. The following morning Charles was up bright and early. He breakfasted and cleared a space for the mirror. He had removed a painting from above the fireplace, one that Mary had bought but he didn't really like it. He was going to send the painting and a few of Mary's other things to the auction house. It was time for a new start and his own collection. At 10 o'clock the doorbell rang. It was the delivery men with his mirror. They kindly put it up in the study for him. He tipped them handsomely.

That evening he was sat in his armchair with a glass of whisky. He looked up at the mirror and sighed. It was a lovely mirror and he felt sure that Mary would have liked it. The clock struck midnight and he decided to retire to bed. He got up and went to switch off the light. As he did so he took one final look at the mirror. There it was again, that face in the bottom corner. He blinked and looked again but it was gone. "I'm just tired" he muttered to himself.

The following morning he took a closer look at the mirror but couldn't see anything. That night just as he switched off the light he again saw the sad face in the mirror. This carried on for two more nights but every morning when he studied the mirror he couldn't see anything wrong. The fifth night he again saw the sad face but instead of switching off the light he went up to it. The face was sad and melancholic and looked imploringly at Charles. He found himself being drawn to the face. As he got up to the mirror a hand reached out and beckoned Charles. He felt an impulse to reach out to the hand and he held his hand up to the mirror. Suddenly he found himself looking out of a room, and saw his study, with the man in the mirror standing there looking back at him. The man said, " Thank you Charles, I have been in tha mirror for many years waiting to be freed. Now it is your turn to look out and reflect on your past and all those people you wrongly convicted in court.

As Charles realised his fate he looked out longingly as the man smiled, turned and left the room.

The Ghost Walk

Mick looked at the poster on the church railings. "Are you brave enough to take the ghost walk?" it said, complete with a brief description of the tour.

"Take a tour through the darkest corners of the city and come face to face with notorious figures from it's gruesome past." The poster went on to explain that a guide, dressed in appropriate Victorian dress would, for a small fee, take tourists around the cathedral and it's environs, encountering various villains and ghosts, played by his colleagues in disguise. Meet by this poster at midnight precisely.

Later that night Mick prepared himself for the cold night excursion. He put on warm winter clothing together with gloves, hat and scarf. Just then the doorbell rang. He answered the door to find three of his friends from the local university where they were all studying.

"Come on Mick what's keeping you?" shouted Jim the smallest of the group. Mick picked up his keys and strolled through the door, slamming it shut behind him.

It was a chilly night but the recent cloud cover had prevented a hard frost from appearing. Just then the cathedral clock struck midnight. Mick and his friends rushed round the corner to the cathedral entrance getting there just in time. A tall thin man, dressed in a black frock coat and typically Victorian black top hat. The black gloves and silver topped cane he carried completed the effect. A small crowd had gathered and were waiting patiently for the tour to start, stamping their feet and clapping their hands to keep warm.

"Welcome gentlemen, you are just in time to join us for the ghost walk" said the guide. "Stay close together I wouldn't like to lose anybody to the dark creatures of the night." He followed this up with a gutteral laugh he had copied from Bela Lugosi in an old Dracula film.

The small group numbered twelve in total; a young courting couple, two elderly couples, two young girls and the four students. They set off down the cathedral close by the side of the cathedral. They passed the Dean's house and turned down a small alleyway that led to a series of steps leading down to a side street.

They stopped at the top of the steps.

"It was here on these steps that Dean Jones, a previous incumbent of the cathedral was brutally murdered back in 1888. His head was neatly severed from his body by an extremely sharp axe that was found next to the body. The head, however, was never found. Just at that moment a man jumped out of the bushes. He wore a dark jacket, cloth cap and baggy trousers. His cap was pulled down low over his eyes. He let out a bloodcurdling scream and held both arms aloft. In one hand he held an axe, dripping with blood, and in the other hand he held a severed head by the hair. The young couple screamed, the girl throwing her arms around her boyfriend. The young girls stood and giggled whilst the two elderly couples looked on in mock horror. The four lads, although expecting something to happen, still jumped with fright at the sudden appearance of the mad axeman. The gruesome figure let out another bloodcurdling scream and fled down the steps.

The tour continued down the churchyard and passed through the graveyard. Mick paused to look at a huge granite angel atop a huge stone slab. It loomed over him like a heavenly apparition. It's eyes seemed to peer at him and into his very soul. He shivered and turned away to follow the group. They had, however gone out of sight so he looked around for them.

He caught sight of a bright light illuminating a gargoyle sat on a tomb in the far corner. He went over for a closer look. As he got closer he realised that it was not a statue but the figure of a man, sat cross-legged on the stone slab. He was dressed in the garb of a Victorian tradesman, corduroy trousers, loose fitting, a collarless shirt and neckerchief. He had a bowler hat on his head. He looked at Mick with great sadness and melancholy. What startled Mick was the deep red gash around his throat, from ear to ear. Blood and sinew dripped from the wound. It's obviously another of the actors he thought to himself.

"Well done old chap, you had me going there for a minute" said Mick.

"He did this to me" said the man. He pointed over to a large well kept vault.

As he said this he sprayed a fine mist over Mick's face.

Mick decided to play along. " Oh yes, and who do you mean exactly?"

"Sir Mortimer Karswell the foreign secretary. He had gotten one of the servant girls pregnant and he had had her killed. He was never caught but I knew his secret and threatened to go to the police unless he paid me to keep silent. He silenced me alright." As he said this Mick felt a fine mist wash over his face, together with a putrid smell from his breath.

Mick was getting a bit worried now.

"I think you're taking your part a bit too seriously mate" said Mick. The figure grabbed hold of Mick by his coat lapels and dragged him closer to him.

" You must help me to set the record straight" cried the figure. Mick was now desperate to get away.

"You can stop the act now, it's gone on for long enough."

The figure screamed out and again his foul breath washed over Mick. He panicked, pulled himself free and ran away to catch up with the others. As he ran away he looked back but the figure had disappeared.

Mick ran and ran until he caught up with the group just as they were leaving the graveyard by the far exit. He bumped into them as he tried to stop himself.

" Where have you been Mick?" asked Jim, one of his friends.

"You missed some really good bits".

Mick ignored him and turned to the tour guide.

"That chap in the far corner of the graveyard was good, he scared the life out of me" he said.

"Where do you mean?" asked the guide.

"On that tomb in the far corner near that big vault."

The guide looked at him puzzled.

"We don't have anyone over there" he said.

"But I saw him sat on a tomb, he spoke to me."

He led the group over to the tomb in question. "What did he say?"" asked the guide. "He went on about a man called Karswell who had supposedly killed a servant girl, and then murdered him to keep him silent."

The guide thought for a moment. "I remember reading something about that in the university library. Karswell was a senior politician and was going to run for prime minister. A servant girl was found murdered in his coal cellar, she was pregnant and had been dead for about a month. The coal man had recently disappeared and it was assumed that he had killed her but nothing was proved."

The group all shivered in fright at this news. Could this figure Mick had seen really have been one of the tour "stooges" and as the guide just winding them up. The guide insisted he was not one of their group.

Mick turned to face the group, the moonlight illuminating his face.

"What's that red stuff on your face Mick?" asked Jim. "It looks like blood."

Mick felt giddy and and thought it probably was blood.

Jim looked at Mick. " You look like you've seen a ghost" he said. Mick thought for a moment and said, " Do you know what, I think I have!"

The Maze

The day dawned bright and clear. Timothy was looking forward to today. He and his mother had booked a day excursion to Burlington Hall. They were going to look around the hall and gardens and then have a picnic by the lake. Timothy had read that they had a huge maze which was notoriously difficult to get out of.

Mother had been up early to make the picnic. She made sandwiches, cheese and pickle, Timothy's favourite. She put some pies, cakes and biscuits in too. She was a good mother to Timothy, she did everything for him. He had never married and never wanted to leave home. She did everything around the house, all the cooking, cleaning and washing. She did all the gardening. Timothy didn't have to lift a finger. His father had left them when he was 11 years old, with the barmaid of the local pub where he spent so much of his free time.

Timothy worked as a clerk at the local solicitor's office. It was a good job, and well paid. He found it quite an easy job. He had worked there since he left school, working his way up from apprentice. He gave most of his wages to mother. He kept a bit back for himself but he didn't really need much. He didn't go out much, he didn't drink or smoke. His mother took care of his money. She was a good housekeeper and had set up a savings account for him, as a nest egg in case anything happened to her.

Timothy was quite happy to stay at home with mother in the evenings. He had his books, he was a keen reader. They often sat and watched tv together in the evenings. They had a holiday at the same time every year, two weeks in a cheap and cheerful bed and breakfast in Cleethorpes. They would trawl around the shops in the morning and sit in deckchairs on the beach in the afternoon. If the weather wasn't nice they would spend the afternoon in the cinema.

All in all Timothy and mother had a good life. They went on the occasional day trip, like this one they were going on, which were organised by the church that they went to every Sunday morning. Timothy was well thought of at the church, especially for staying at home with his mother and tipping up his wages to her. She did everything for him and she never complained. Which is as it should be seeing as he was the breadwinner, it was her job to look after him.

Mother took a job as a cleaner when his father left home. It was at the solicitor's where he worked. She had asked for an apprentice job for Timothy when he left school. He had worked his way up to chief clerk. Now it was mother's turn to stay at home and be provided for, which he did to the best of his ability. He had a lot to be grateful to mother for, he had a good home life.

They set off from home at 9 o'clock. They walked down the street to the church hall where everybody was gathered waiting for the coach. The coach turned up and they all got on board. These church trips were always well supported and the coach was full as they set off. The driver took them down long winding country lanes and eventually they arrived at Burlington Hall. Off they went, Timothy and mother, into the hall. They enjoyed looking around the grand rooms and all the lovely furniture and paintings. Afterwards they went out into the gardens to find a shady spot for lunch. He didn't like sitting in the sun as he always went red and burnt easily.

They ate their lunch and then mother said she was going to have forty winks in the sun. She got up and left him under the tree. Timothy looked over to the maze entrance and saw a group waiting to go in. They had to follow the guide as it was notoriously difficult a maze to navigate alone. He rushed over to join them. Mother would be alright without him for now he thought. He just missed the group as they entered the maze. Nevermind, he thought, I'll soon catch them up and in he went. He had heard that the guide would leave a piece of string to trace the route back out in case anyone got lost, so he wasn't worried. He entered the maze and turned left. He could hear voices and so he knew he was going the right way, he was just behind them. He hurried to the next corner but had just missed them. He looked and found the piece of string so he knew he was going the right way. Every time he rounded a corner he just missed the tour guide. He hurried but still couldn't catch them. He eventually reached the centre but again he had missed the tour. He decided to sit for a minute and get his breath back.

He must have nodded off as the next thing he knew the sun was burning his face. He looked at his watch, it said three o'clock. He couldn't believe it. He would have to get a move on to get back to mother before the coach left at four. There would just be time for one of mother's cakes and a drink. He remembered to look for the string, and sure enough there it was. He followed it but it led back to the centre. He tried again but it led him back to the centre. This can't be right he thought He started to panic and shouted as loud as he could but nobody answered. He was getting frantic but then he thought mother would come looking for him. She wouldn't leave without him. He sat back down on the bench and soon nodded off again in the warm sun.

Back on the coach mother had a smile on her face. What a good day she had, especially now she had got rid of that prat of a son of hers. At sixty it wasn't easy for her to wait hand and foot on that lazy good for nothing lad. He expected far too much and never lifted a finger to help her. He treated the place as a hotel and her as some kind of slave. Well not any more. She would be able to start living for herself.

She could travel around the world and be waited on for a change. It had been quite easy really. She had followed Timothy into the maze. When he fell asleep in the centre she had simply laid some string in a circular route around the maze and back to the centre. As she retraced her steps she removed the tour guide's string so that their was no way of getting out. By the time they found him he would either be mad or dead from heat exhaustion. He never could stand the heat. And so it was. They found him during the last tour of the evening. By the she would be back home and acting all innocent. Nobody would suspect a thing. She had been planning this for quite a while and just had to wait for the right opportunity.

As she sat having a cool drink on the seafront at Marbella, she took out a copy of the local newspaper she brought from home. In it was a report that a a man had been found in a maze. He had been badly sunburnt and his skin was all blistered. He had gone completely insane and all he could say was "Where's mother, where's mother."

She smile to herself. "I'm here Timothy, I'm here"

The Unknown Soldier

The day dawned bright and clear, just a hint of autumn in the air as General Henry Davies walked around the village of Milchester. He was doing his morning rounds before he went to his committee meeting about the village green. They were to discuss plans for a war memorial there to commemorate the lads killed in the First World War. This didn't altogether sit well with the General. He had commanded a battalion of local lads during the war. Some of them were not fit to be put on the memorial, that's what he thought. They didn't like taking orders, were lazy and not well disciplined. If it wasn't for him none of them would have gone "over the top". Backbone, that's what they lacked. If I had my way there would be no memorial.

The general was one of the old school. He had been raised by his nanny, and then went on to boarding school. He hardly knew his parents. Then he went to university and then straight into the army. That had made him into the man he was, he thought. In truth he was an overbearing, pompous buffoon.

Henry had never married, never had much time for women. They had their place in society of course. As long as they knew their place, in the home, then he could put up with them. It was a man's world and they had better get used to it.

It was after the war that he came to live

in the village. He had been looking for somewhere nice and quiet where he could take charge on all the village committees, somewhere he could be in charge, just like in his army days.

So it was that he came to live in Milchester. There was enough to keep him occupied. He was on the church committee, the council and also the school board. He was one of the governors. On top of that he was on the committee for what was known as village watch, looking around the village and making sure everyone was safe and strangers were closely watched. All in all he was satisfied with village life here. It was his village and nothing happened that he didn't either know about or had approved. The villagers respected him, well they feared him which suited him nicely.

It was on a bright sunny morning that he found himself walking around his village when he spotted a stranger It was a young man in army uniform, like the one his regiment had worn during the war. At first he thought it was just his imagination. He had difficulty sleeping, the horrors of the war kept coming back to haunt him. He had a few glasses of whisky in the pub every night before retiring, hoping to keep the demons at bay. He would usually get a few hours sleep before the demons appeared and he often woke up in a cold sweat. He would get up early and have a good breakfast of kidneys, eggs and bacon. After that he was back to his old self again. He would then read his morning paper. Then he would leave his butler to clear up behind him while he went on his morning patrol around the village. And so here he was, keeping tabs on the stranger, the soldier that was walking around his village. He had to be quick and sort out this problem. He had to get down to the church hall for a council meeting about the proposed war memorial. He thought it a complete waste of money but he couldn't say that. Many of the villagers had lost relatives during the war and if he went against them he could lose his position in the village. So he quickly followed the soldier. He lost him as he turned behind the pub, he couldn't see him anywhere. He searched everywhere but the soldier was nowhere to be seen. He looked at his pocket watch and saw that it was time for the meeting so he returned to the village hall. The meeting got underway and the war memorial was approved and plans set up for raising the money needed. Before the meeting broke up Henry asked everyone if they had seen the soldier in the village. Nobody had seen him and nobody had a relative in the army, and all the soldiers had been demobbed last year so he couldn't be a local. He left the meeting feeling frustrated. What was going on in the village. He took his committee business very seriously much to the amusement and annoyance of the other villagers. The kids had a nickname for him. Here comes Hawkeye they would say as they saw him on one of his patrols. They often hid until he had passed on. He had sometimes clipped them around the ear for no good reason. He would just say know your place and walk on.

He got back home just in time for lunch. His butler had it all set up for him. He would eat lunch and then sit in his armchair in the study with a glass of whisky and a book. He wolud often nod off for an hour or two. He would have dinner at 6 o'clock, no later or it would play havoc with his indigestion. Then at 8 o'clock precisely he would go to the village pub for a glass or two of his favourite malt whisky. He didn't have too many as he liked to be in control. At precisely 10.30pm he would make his way back home. That was his routine.

The following morning he was up and dressed. He had breakfast as usual. He had a meeting with the vicar. Lady Mary wanted him to do a reading at the funeral service of her late husband, Lord Mortimer. Seeing as he was now the senior in rank in the village it was right that he should give the reading he thought to himself. As he was doing his rounds before meeting the vicar, he saw the soldier again. The soldier saw Henry and turned towards him and smiled. Henry thought for a minute that he knew that face. The soldier turned away and walked quickly away. Henry decided to follow him. He ran after him and followed him as he left the village. Again, despite his best efforts, he lost sight of the soldier.

He was late for his meeting with the vicar

so he hurried back to the church. He asked the vicar about the soldier but he hadn't seen him at all. Nobody else had seen him and it was quite a mystery. He was determined to solve the mystery.

The following morning it was drizzling but that wasn't going to stop Henry from doing his rounds. He set off as usual and hadn't got far before he again saw the soldier. He shouted to him but the solider smiled and walked on. He followed the unknown soldier to the village green. The soldier turned and beckoned to Henry to follow him, and so he did. The soldier left the village and walked into the middle of a large flat field. He stopped and waited for Henry to catch up with him. Henry caught up with him and asked who he was. As the soldier turned round Henry recognised him as one of his men who had been posted as missing in action. "Welcome, General, you are now trapped in no man's land just like you left us in no man's land in France. You should have led us back to safety but you threatened to shoot anyone who turned back. Now it's your turn to be stuck out in the middle of nowhere." The soldier then disappeared. Shaken Henry started to walk back to the village but as he got to the edge of the field his feet stuck firmly to the ground. He tried another way and again his feet stopped him from leaving the field. He spent the next two hours trying to leave the field but couldn't. He just sat down and cried for his nanny.

Neat And Tidy

Arthur Groves was a successful businessman. He was a confirmed bachelor. He was now in his mid fifties. He was having lunch with his old school friend Guy, at their club. It was a gentleman's club with old fashioned values. As they ate their lunch Arthur turned to Guy and broke the news.

"I'm getting married next week"

Guy looked at him in surprise. "Marrying who?"

"Eleanor, Charles Bunting's daughter."

"Well I never, you the eternal bachelor getting married. I hope she can cope with your precise ways Arthur!"

Arthur and Eleanor were married and settled into Arthur's bungalow that he had lived in for many years. It was a very modern bungalow with all modern conveniences.

Arthur returned home from work at five every evening. He would pour himself a glass of whisky, put on a Brahms CD and settle into his favourite armchair. He would have a read of his Times newspaper. Tonight was no exception. He got a glass out of the cocktail cabinet and put it on the top surface. He poured a good measure of whisky, put the bottle back in it's proper place and picked up the glass. He looked carefully at the bar top and wiped a wet mark made by the glass. He went over to his favourite armchair and sat down. He put the glass on to a coaster on the little table on the left hand side of the chair. He sat back and listened to the music. He reached down on the right side of the chair to pick up his newspaper from the Canterbury, a small wooden magazine rack. He felt around but couldn't find it. He looked down and there was no Canterbury. He glanced around the room and saw it over by the television.

"Eleanor..... Eleanor!"

Eleanor came in from the bedroom .

"Eleanor, you've moved the furniture around!"

"Yes I have, I thought it looked better that way." she answered.

"But I can't find anything!"

"Well if it bothers you I can always put it back" she replied.

That evening they went into the bedroom. Eleanor got into bed whilst Arthur took a shower in the en-suite bathroom. He eventually came out in his dressing gown. He reached into the chest of drawers for a pair of underpants but only found his wife's things.

"Eleanor, where are my pants?"

Oh I put them in the drawers on your side of the bed, it seemed better that way."

"Eleanor my pants have always been in that set of drawers, left hand side, third drawer down."

He beckoned her to get out of bed and follow him. "Come with me".

They went into the kitchen and to the door that led to the cellar. He switched on the lights and they went down the stairs.

" Now this is my workshop. I come down here to relax. I have everything in order."

He pointed to a wall where there were shelves full of jars each one labelled with it's contents.

"Look here , a row of jars with nails, all sizes, in ascending order. Here a row of jars with screws, again in ascending order, with sub groups for type of screw. Everything in it's place and a place for everything."

There was also a board on the wall next to it with saws, hammers and screwdrivers all neatly hanging on hooks.

"I can lay my hand on what I want without even looking up. Now do you see the benefit of order?"

Eleanor just nodded. They left the cellar and went back into the sitting room.

The following evening Arthur decided to cook a special meal for Eleanor. He was going to cook spaghetti bolognese. He put an apron on, he wanted to keep his shirt clean and tidy. He opened the cupboard and reached in for a tin of tomato puree. He couldn't find one. He looked for a tin of tomatoes but again he couldn't find one. He looked at the chart he had stuck on the inside of the cupboard doors.

"That's funny we should have three of each. He looked for tins of beans, again there were none but the list said two.

"Eleanor, would you come into the kitchen please."

Eleanor walked in. "Yes dear" she asked.

"Eleanor why are there no tins of tomatoes in the cupboard? The chart says three."

She looked puzzled for a moment and then said. "Oh I must have forgotten to get some more, sorry Arthur."

Arthur was getting more and more worked up.

" Eleanor you must follow our system. This is a list on the door of all the tins we have, and against them are three pencil marks. When you use a tin you simply rub out one of the marks and then buy some when you next go shopping. But look at this, three tins of tomato puree, but no tomato puree. Three tins of tomatoes but no tomatoes. Eleanor you simply haven't bothered!! How can you expect everything to run smoothly when you don't follow the system. I can't live with this chaos."

The following morning Arthur got out of bed, showered and dressed. Eleanor was already up and making breakfast. He walked into the kitchen to find the table set up perfectly, knives and forks in the correct order and napkins carefully folded. There was a pot of coffee ready and the cooked breakfast was all set out on his plate.

" I say Eleanor this is simply marvelous. Just what I need, I've got a busy day ahead of me. I'll be back at six o'clock dear. He ate his breakfast, drank his coffee, kissed his wife goodbye and set off for the city.

Eleanor washed the breakfast dishes, did all the cleaning and made sure everything was spotless. She looked around to make sure everything was in it's right place. When she was satisfied she had her lunch. In the afternoon she listened to some classical music and sat to read a magazine. She was feeling bored and so she got up, went to the cocktail cabinet and poured herself a gin and tonic. She walked over to her chair and sat down. She put the glass down on the coffee table. She felt restless and got up to look out of the window at the large garden. She went to the coffee table and picked up her glass. She was horrified to notice that the glass had left a wet ring on the table. She glanced at the clock, quarter to six. She rushed over to the cocktail cabinet to get a coaster. As she wrestled to get one out of the pack they all fell out on to the floor. Eleanor put the glass on the coaster and then went down into the cellar to get a bottle of furniture polish. She knelt down by the table and poured some of the liquid polish onto a cloth and put the bottle on the floor. As she polished the table her foot caught the bottle which spilled onto the carpet. She frantically tried to mop it up but she couldn't remove the stain. She got up and headed for the kitchen. As she did this she caught a painting on the wall with her hand, and it fell onto the floor. Eleanor picked it up and went to hang it up but the hook had come out of the wall.

Eleanor looked at the clock, it was now five minutes to six. She hurried down into the cellar. She reached for a jar on the shelf, opened it and shook out the contents. They were screws. She opened a second jar and tipped the contents on the table, these were bolts. She saw a little cabinet on the table with small draws. She pulled open the top drawer and the whole cabinet fell over, spilling various nails all over the table and floor. She picked up a nail. All she needed now was a hammer. There were three hammers hanging on the board on the wall. She yanked one out of it's fitting and the whole board fell off the wall, throwing tools all over the place.

Eleanor picked up the hammer and nail and reached the bottom step out of the cellar when she saw Arthur on the top step.

"Eleanor what are you doing , you've messed up the whole house!"

He went down the steps and inspected the damage. Eleanor climbed a couple of stairs so she was just above Arthur. She looked down at him and held up the hammer and nail.

" I just needed a nail to hang up a picture." she said.

Arthur looked up at her.

"Eleanor can't you do anything neatly? Can't you, can't you do anything neatly, can't you, can't you, can't you do anything neatly?"

His voice went on and on and Eleanor couldn't take it anymore, she began to get hysterical. She raised the hammer above her head and brought it down on Arthur's skull. He collapsed in a pool of blood.

A couple of hours later and the cellar workshop was looking neat and tidy again. Eleanor surveyed her handiwork.

" Well Arthur I have managed to do something neatly after all. A place for everything and everything in it's place. Yes everything is neat and tidy Arthur."

She looked at the rows of jars neatly arranged on the shelves. Each one neatly labelled, eyes, ears, nose,teeth, heart, etc.

"Yes Arthur you are neat and tidy, a place for everything and everything in it's place! And she laughed.

The Tower

Helen had always wanted to visit Tuscany in Italy. The place simply fascinated her. She finally got her wish and could now afford to go there. She hired a villa for two weeks. She was going to hire a car and visit as many places as she could and sample some of the local cuisine and of course the Chianti wine. She had taken her trusty guidebook with her and selected places she had to visit. First on her list was a trip to Florence. She spent the day looking around the museums and galleries. She visited the cathedral and climbed to the top of the dome which gave wonderful views of the surrounding countryside. She would sit at a pavement cafe and just watch the world go by. She also visited Pisa and marvelled at the famous leaning tower. It leaned at an alarming angle that the photos didn't do justice to.

Next was a trip to Siena famous for it's shell-shaped piazza where the Palio, the medieval horse race was run. She also went to the small town of Vinci, where Leonardo was born. There was a museum dedicated to his inventions and theories.

One afternoon she glanced through her guidebook and found a photograph of a large imposing tower. She read the blurb about it. It was perched on a hilltop overlooking the Chianti vineyards. Apparently it was used as a prison for some time and was closed suddenly in 1752. There was also a legend that said if anyone climbed the 350 steps to the top of the tower alone were never seen again.

"What a fascinating place" she thought. " I really must visit that". A quick glance at her map told her it was only 20 kilometres away so she decided to go there straight away.

It was late afternoon when she got her first glimpse of the tower. It was a large imposing structure made of stone. It dominated the skyline. There was a small car park at the foot of the tower but there was nobody there, only Helen.

Helen got out of her car and took her guide book with her. She strolled over to the tower entrance. There was a notice by the door explaining, in several languages, how many steps there were to the top of the tower and the old legend about those who climbed to the top alone never being seen again.

" I'm not scared of a silly superstition like that" she muttered to herself.

She pushed open the old heavy wooden door and went in. It was quite dark in the entrance and felt cool. There were small windows situated at regular intervals in the wall that gave just enough light to see by. A small handrail had been thoughtfully provided to help the weary visitors on the long climb.

Helen began to climb the steps. After about fifty steps she saw a plaque on the wall explaining how a prisoner had thrown himself to his death out of this window as he was being taken to the cell at the top.

Helen looked out of the window at the vine covered hillside.

At the 200th step Helen stopped again for a rest. On the wall was yet another plaque jokingly stating that anyone who went beyond this point did so at their own risk. A voice in Helen's head told her to go back but she refused to be beaten by silly superstitions. She climbed on.

Finally she reached step three hundred and fifty. This top step ended by a small wooden door that opened out onto a viewing platform that ran around the whole of the tower. Helen went through the door and out onto the platform. Dusk was fast descending as she tentatively looked down from the tower.

"This can't be right, I seem to be way too high for only three hundred and fifty step" she thought. Sure enough she could hardly make out her own car down below.

" It must be some sort of optical illusion" she thought. She gazed out of the darkening countryside.

Tentatively she passed back through the wooden door to the staircase. An overwhelming sense of foreboding washed over her as she took her first step down. She panicked and sat down.

" I can't go down" she cried. Slowly Helen got up and started down the steps. She counted as she did so.

"One, two, three..."

She halted at one hundred and fifty steps, by the plaque that jokingly advised tourists to go back down.

"Good only another two hundred steps to go." She carried on. There was still a nagging doubt in her mind about reaching the bottom.

"Don't be stupid just keep going and you'll soon reach the bottom."

At three hundred steps down she stopped and looked out of one of the windows.

"This can't be right, I'm still far too high up. I don't look any closer to the ground than I did at two hundred steps." Sure enough the ground seemed a very long way off considering she was now only fifty steps from the ground.

Dusk was rapidly descending and it was getting darker in the tower. Helen began to panic, her breathing deepened and her heartbeat quickened.

"Three hundred and forty nine, three hundred and fifty!" This should have been the bottom of the tower but the steps carried on downwards. Helen carried on, thinking she had counted wrong.

"Four hundred and fifty!" She looked out of the window and saw she was still no nearer to the ground.

"What's going on!" she cried.

Gradually she remembered the old legend. Wearily she carried on, despair in her voice as she counted..

"Five hundred and fifty, five hundred and fifty one, five hundred and fifty two...."

The Cyclist

Gary arrived at the starting line. It was the 6th May. There was still a slight chill in the early morning air but that didn't bother him as he was very confident that he would win the race. He had won it for the last three years and he was going to win it again. It was a 120 mile race around Yorkshire, starting at Hebden Bridge and finishing in Whitby. He had his route sheet but he didn't need it. He always made his own route. That was why he always won. He would race off the front for the first 20 miles or so, making sure nobody could see him. He then went off course. He was always first to finish and nobody was any the wiser.

He had a point to prove to his fellow cyclists and teammates. A few years ago his team had won a place in the Tour De France. Every rider was put through his paces and training was tough. Gary had trained really hard and was confident that he would be included in the team. He had trained on the hills and on his time trialling skills and although not the best he was very good and was improving all the time.

Selection day arrived and Gary lined up with the other riders. The team list for the Tour De France was read out. Gary was shocked to discover he was not on the list. They said he wasn't good enough which he couldn't really believe. He felt he was better than most of the other riders.

He later found out that the rider selected instead of him just happened to be the president's nephew. The president was responsible for the rise of the club. He had invested a fortune of his own money into the club and so he wanted something in return. It was a bitter pill to swallow as he knew he was good enough for the Tour.

Of course they didn't do very well in the Tour De France and Gary knew that he could have won a stage in the Tour. The rest of the team never mentioned the Tour after that but Gary never forgot the insult.

And so here he was, still racing for the club. He was determined to win everything and show them how good he was. He began well, winning quite a few races, and winning many trophies and medals. However, he was finding it harder now and so he came to the decision to win at all costs.

Here he was at 8am on the 6th May at the start line in Hebden Bridge. There were about 60 riders and he knew many of them. He looked over at them and they nodded in recognition. Many of the cyclists there knew Gary well, and most thought he was too arrogant and cocky. They all knew the story of him losing his team place to the president's nephew in the Tour De France and although they didn't really like him, they felt some sympathy with him.

He had won every race so far this season and many other riders were beginning to get suspicious of Gary although they couldn't prove anything. Nobody could understand how he could race off so quickly at the start and yet be fresh at the finish line.

They lined up at the start and before long they were off. As usual Gary raced off the front and disappeared out of sight of the others. This was where he would put his plan in action. He had done his homework before the race, as usual and he knew where the train station was. He arrived there in time for the next train. He got on it and went to Whitby. He got off the train and went for some lunch. He even went to the cinema to see a film. When the time was right he would head out into the countryside and get ready to ride to the finish. He got on his bike, clipped into his pedals and set off. By the time the finish line arrived he had worked up quite a sweat to make it look realistic. He crossed the line and took the victory salute. He tried to slow down but he couldn't. The pedals kept spinning round and wouldn't let him slow down. He tried to unclip from the pedals but again they wouldn't let him. He rode through the finish and disappeared out of Whitby. He shouted at passers by to help him but they all ignored him. He kept pedalling throughout the rest of the day. No matter what he did he couldn't stop pedalling and he couldn't unclip from his pedals. It was as if his bike had had enough of his cheating and wanted to teach him a lesson.

The race organisers didn't know what to make of Gary's disappearing act but seeing as how he wasn't very popular nobody was too bothered They decided to give the victory to the runner up. There was always the suspicion that Gary was a cheat and so they disqualified him anyway. Nobody gave him a second though, not until they saw the newspaper article a few days later.

It was a report in the Scottish Herald newspaper that a cyclist matching Gary's description, was found in a ditch in a remote part of the highlands. His feet were still attached to his pedals. He was suffering from complete physical and mental exhaustion. His legs had suffered badly. Nearly every bone in his legs were broken. It was unlikely that he would ever walk again. Gary had ridden his last race.

The Vicarage

Patsy and Charlie were on their way to pick up the keys to what was going to be their "forever" home. It was a seven bedroom, two reception room detached house, with a large garden. It was located in the heart of the village of Pennington. It was an old vicarage that used to belong to the village church just down the road. They had built a new, modern vicarage next to the church which was more convenient for the new vicar. This was an absolute bargain. It had been on the market for three years and the locals took no interest in it. It was a bit run down but they didn't mind that, they could modernize it just how they wanted it. They had three children, two boys and a girl, with another on the way, so a big house was just what they needed.

They had just been to the solicitor's to sign the last of the paperwork and were now going to the estate agents to pick up the keys. They were keen to get started on the renovations and hopefully finish before Christmas when the new baby was due.

Charlie and his brother Mick were quite good at renovating houses, they were both builders and had done that sort of work for others. Now it was time to do it for themselves. They could get all the materials they needed at trade prices and so save a fortune there. They had been through the house and made a list of what needed doing and what they needed.

They had made a cheeky low offer for the old vicarage as soon as they had sold their own house. They couldn't believe that it had been accepted without hesitation. Of course it was meant to be, thought Patsy, a new start and their dream home.

They had made enquiries about the old vicarage and discovered it had been empty for quite some time before being put up for sale. The last vicar had lost the plot after he caught his wife with the verger. Apparently he had kicked her out and the verger, but nobody actually saw them leave. He kept custody of their two daughters, one 14 and the other 16. His wife never argued with him.

The vicar had become a "hellfire and brimstone" preacher and, according to the old dear who lived across the road, he became very peculiar. He kept the girls out of sight and apart from his sermons he was very rarely seen in public. One of his daughters left suddenly to live in Cumbria with a distant relative. Eventually the other daughter went to join her. Nobody actually saw them leave.

Not long after the vicar announced he was also leaving and joining his family in Cumbria. Nothing was ever heard from them again. The vicarage was never used after that as the new vicar had charge of three parishes and stayed in another vicarage. Eventually they got their own vicar and had a new vicarage built for him, nearer to the church and less costly to run.

Two weeks before Christmas the house was finally ready. They had fitted new windows throughout, rewired the house and put in a new bathroom and kitchen. There was only their bedroom and the attic left to do but they could wait until after Christmas. Patsy wanted all fitted wardrobes and that would take time so they left it until the last.

Monday morning finally arrived, moving day. They hoped the rain would hold off long enough to get their furniture in the new house. The 2 boys were at school and Patsy was looking after their daughter Harriet. Come lunchtime and they went to the local chippy for fish and chips. When they had finished they decided to take a look at the cellar. They wondered what they could do with it. Charlie looked at his watch. It was time to pick up the boys from school. As he turned to go up the cellar steps he noticed a newish patch of plaster on one of the walls, fresher than that all around it. There was also a part of the wall that seemed crudely built, compared to the rest. Never mind, he thought, he could sort that out later.

It was 11 o'clock that night when they finally got into bed, tired but happy. The kids were fast asleep and everthing was nice and quiet. This is perfect thought Patsy as she drifted off to sleep. She was stirred by a slight tapping noise coming from the wall at the end of the bed. There it was again, and then all was quiet. They woke in the morning to find that snow had fallen. There would be no school today and no work for Charlie, not that he had much on lately, just a few odd jobs and some decorating. Patsy mentioned to Charlie the tapping on the wall she heard. He said it was probably the old fireplace that was bricked up and it was most likely a bird that had got trapped there after going down the chimney. He said he would look at it when he came to decorate the bedroom.

The day was spent unpacking the rest of their stuff. It was starting to look more like home now. The kids were out playing in the snow. That evening as they all went to bed, Patsy listened for the tapping noise. She heard nothing and was just drifting off to sleep when there it was again, a gentle tap tap tapping. After a few minutes it stopped.

Patsy told Charlie about it the following morning. He promised he would look at it as soon as Christmas was out of the way. It was less than two weeks away and it was going to be a big job getting the fitted wardrobes just how Patsy wanted. That night as they went to bed, Charlie lay there listening for the tapping noise but heard nothing. He did the same thing for the next two nights but again nothing. Patsy thought maybe it was just her imagination working overtime.

Christmas came and went but still Charlie hadn't started on the bedroom. Then one evening Patsy heard the tap tap tapping noise from behind the wall. This time it went on longer, and then suddenly stopped. She again told Charlie and he agreed to investigate.

That night they both heard the tapping noise. Charlie got up early the next morning and made a start. He began to strip the walls. The following night the tapping got louder and lasted for much longer. Charlie finally stripped the wall where the old fireplace used to be. It had been crudely bricked up, and fairly recently by the look of it. That night the tapping was accompanied by a scraping sound and it went on for quite some time.

The next morning Charlie decided to break down the wall that was in the fireplace. He took a sledgehammer to it. As the bricks began to fall he could see something behind the wall. He called Patsy to come and take a look. As they finally removed the last bricks they were shocked at what they saw. There, chained up to the wall was the remains of a human being. The flesh was almost completely gone. There were remants of a dress on the body.

The police and forensic team finally left the house late that evening. They had been able to identify the body as the vicar's wife. She hadn't run off with the verger after all. The vicar had bricked her up behind the fireplace alive. But what happened to the verger? He had also disappeared.

That evening as they lay in bed, Patsy and Charlie heaved a huge sigh of relief as the nightmare discovery was finally put behind them. There were no more sounds of tapping and scraping. The kids had seen it all as a fascinating story, one they could tell to all their friends at school, who would no doubt be very jealous.

Things settled down again and life went on as normal. A couple of weeks later, Patsy woke up in the night and went down to the kitchen for a drink. She was having a nightmare and woke up with a start to find her mouth very dry. As she sipped the glass of water she heard a sound. She stood still and listened. It was the same tap tap tapping noise she had heard in the bedroom but this was coming from the cellar. She suddenly remembered that the police said they couldn't trace the verger....

Comrades In Arms

Harry was sitting in his trench on the Somme battlefield in France. It was June 1916 and something big was in the air. The artillery had fired a non stop barrage on the German trenches for the last seven days, in preparation for the big push.

Harry had joined up in early 1915. He had rushed to the recruiting office in his town, together with all his pals from the mill where they worked. They were all good Lancashire lads, hard working lads. They had gone through months of basic training and route marches and now they were considered ready to do their bit. They had crossed over from Dover to Boulogne on the French coast. From there it was a series of marches to get to the support trenches near their allotted sector. They had spent the first night in France, in the support trenches. The following morning they were moved up to the front line trenches ready for the attack. They could hear the large guns firing relentlessly over their heads. The officers had said it would be a walk over as nothing could survive such a barrage and all the German trenches would have been destroyed.

And so here he was, with all his pals around him. It was comforting to know that they were there and they all said they would look out for each other. They were waiting for the final signal to send them "over the top."

Their officer came down the line offering words of advice and encouragement. Their sergeants barked out the order to fix bayonets and all along the trench was the sound of scraping blades coming out of their scabbards and the click as they slotted onto the rifle. Some, nervous of what lay ahead, fumbled with their bayonets. Harry helped his nearest pal Bill to fix his bayonet. They just exchanged nervous smiles.

All of a sudden the sound of officer's whistles filled the still air and they were off. Harry climbed up the ladder and immediately heard the chatter of the German machine guns. They would open for short bursts, pause and then start again. He saw a line of men in front of him all drop down. He crouched as low as he could. All around him he could hear the shouts and screams of injured men. His officer was in front blowing his whistle and beckoning them on with his revolver in his hand. Harry crouched and ran as fast as he could, hearing the zip of bullets flying past him.

Eventually he saw a bomb crater up ahead and he dropped into it. There were several others in there, including his pal Bill. Casualties seemed quite heavy. Harry had passed many injured and dying men as he ran, but he couldn't stop to help them. One of their sergeants joined them in the bomb crater. They had drifted to the left in the advance and it seemed quieter here. The sergeant got them together and they made a rush for the German trench literally yards in front of them. There was no machine gun fire just rifle fire from the trench. They jumped down into the trench amongst the German soldiers. There was a fierce hand to hand fight going on with the lads bayonetting most of the Germans. It was at this point that Harry was hit on the head and he collapsed unconcious.

When he came around the rest of the lads had gone. He didn't know wether they had gone forward or had retreated. It was fairly quiet now. He became aware of a low groaning sound coming from around the corner of the trench. He carefully stepped over the dead bodies and peered around the corner. On the ground lay a German soldier. He was clutching his chest. There was blood on his uniform and it was seeping through his hands. He looked pitifully at Harry. He lifted his hand in desperation. Harry felt sorry for the German and went over to him. " Sorry chum but there's nothing I can do for you" he said. The German moaned and clutched his chest again. Harry sat there looking at him for over an hour. He give him some water to drink.

Finally he could bear it no more and he climbed out of the trench. It was strangely quiet and he managed to get back to his own trenches in relative safety. Eventually his conscience got the better of him and he went to the sergeant. He pleaded with him to send a stretcher party out to help the wounded German. Eventually they agreed and Harry led them over no man's land back to the German trench. The wounded soldier was still alive, but only just. They got him onto the stretcher and carefully carried him back to their own lies. They took him to the field hospital. The surgeon took one look at him and made him a priority. " We need to operate on this chap straight away" he said, "He is only just hanging on."

Two hours later and Harry went back to the hospital to see how he was doing. " You did well to get him back here alive" said the surgeon. " He would have certainly died within hours if you hadn't.

The German slowly recovered and he was put into a camp of other German prisoners who were going to be exchanged for British prisoners. As they were being led away Harry went over to him to shake his hand. The German could speak no English but one of his fellow soldiers could, and so he acted as an interpreter. The German thanked him for saving his life and said he would never forget his British friend Harry. Harry asked what his name was. He replied "Adolf". "What is your surname so I can keep in touch?" he asked. The answer came back. "My name is Hitler, Adolf Hitler, and thank you very much for saving my life."

The Miner

Gareth Jones was working the night shift tonight. His mind was elsewhere as he was going down the shaft in the cage. He and his team he was working with were going to a new part of the mine. There were five of them altogether.. They were working at the far end of the mine. There job was to break through to the coal seam and then another team would take over digging out the coal. They would then go down one of the various tunnels to a new part and start again. It was a vast mine with many long tunnels that stretched for miles underground.

Gareth had been working in the mines for the last seven years, since he was fourteen. It was a tough job but he was following in the family traditions. His father and grandfather both worked in the mines. His father had been killed in a mining accident three years ago. He had left behind a wife and six children. Gareth and his three brothers all worked down the mine. His brothers were all married and had children of their own. Gareth still lived at home with his mother and two younger sisters, and so he was now the breadwinner.

The year was 1914 and most of the young men in the village where they lived had joined up and were fighting in France. The rest were all down the pit. Gareth saw the war as a great adventure and often wished he was over there in the fresh air and sushine. When he mentioned joining up his mother would break down in tears afraid that he would never come back. Two of his older brothers did join up and they went over to France.

And so Gareth got up at 3am to go and do another long hard shift at the mine, a job he hated with a passion. He was working in a particularly dangerous part of the mine with his closest friend, Edwin Edwards, when they heard a rumble and before they knew it the roof had collapsed on top of them. Luckily the pit props had held up some of the earth and coal and they were not buried. Gareth looked over at Edwin and saw he was out cold. He crawled over to him and shook him, trying to bring him round. Edwin's legs had been crushed by a falling rock and there was no way he could walk out. Gareth decided to try and reach the cage and get help. He began to clear the debris and soon found that it wasn't as bad as he thought. The rest of the tunnel was clear. He went back to Edwin and gently lifted him up. He slowly limped back to the cage, about a mile away, until he came to the cage. He managed to get Edwin up to the surface. He was rushed to hospital where he had to have both legs amputated. That was it for Edwin.

Gareth made his mind up there and then that he was going to join the army. Without telling his mother, he just left a note, he went to the recruiting office and signed up. After his initial training he was sent with his battalion over to France.

When he finally got to the front line he discovered it was much worse than he could ever have imagined. There were shells bursting all around them and the occasional ping of a sniper's bullet overhead. The army made use of his mining skills to dig tunnels under the wire to the German lines.

The fighting continued for months until orders came up that his battalion were going "over the top". Gareth was nervous but glad to at least be above ground again. At 1400 hours came the order to climb out of the trenches. They rushed forward amnogst a hail of bullets from machine gun fire. The artillery shells were bursting all around them and smoke filled the air, making it very difficult for them to see where they were going. Men all around him were dropping down , hit by the bullets. Thet got the call to put on their gask masks, which hampered their view. Gareth could hardly see or breath in the mask and amidst the smoke. He stumbled on not really knowing where he was going. He couldn't see any of his pals and began to get scared and feel alone.

Suddenly he felt a hand grasp his hand. He couldn't see who it was in the smoke. They stumbled back towards their own lines. Gareth stumbled and fell. The stranger picked him up and carried him onwards.

Eventually they reached their own lines. The stranger took Gareth to the nearest field hospital. He gingerly put him down on a bed and walked off, never looking back. Gareth looked at the stranger as he walked off and thought there was something familiar about him. Must be one of his pals from the battalion, he thought.

Gradually he came around and asked the orderly if the stranger was still around so he could thank him. The orderly went off to find out. He eventually came back. "No I am sorry but he has disappeared. He did leave this note for you though."

Gareth took the note and read it.

" You helped me in my hour of need down that mine, and saved my life. Now it is my turn to do the same for you. Your lifelong friend,"

                Edwin   Edwards

Printed in Great Britain
by Amazon.co.uk, Ltd.,
Marston Gate.